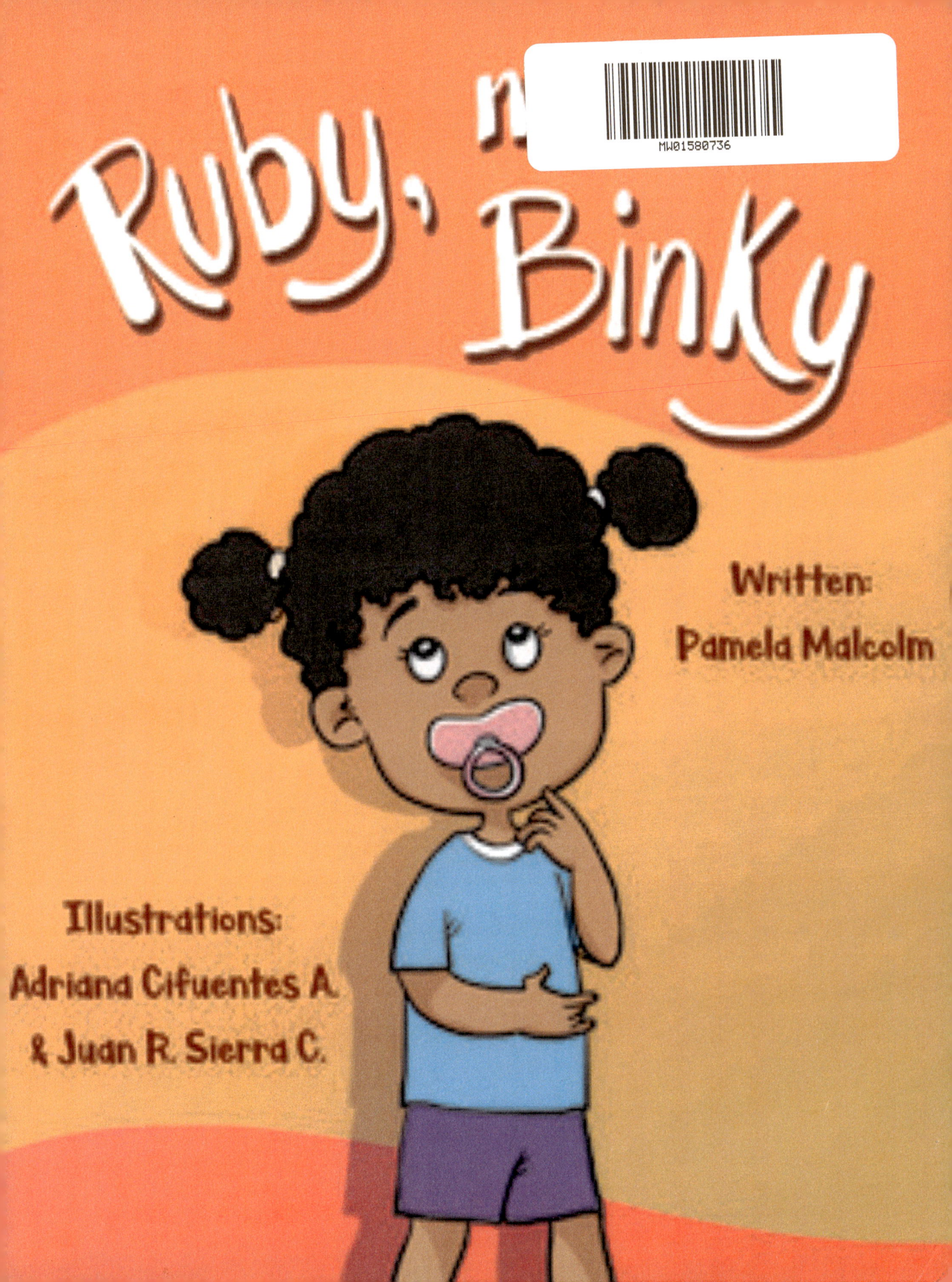

Ruby No More Binky

By Pamela Malcolm

This is a work of fiction. The characters and events described herein are imaginary and are not intended to refer to specific places or to living persons alive or dead.

All rights reserved.
This book or parts thereof may not be reproduced, distributed or transmitted in any form by any means—electronic, mechanical, photocopy, recording, or otherwise—without prior written permission of the publisher, except as provided by United States of America copyright law.
For permission requests, write to the publisher.

Copyright © April 2018 by Pamela Malcolm
Aryla Publishing

For my little Ruby

If you enjoy this book I would love it if you could leave me feedback.

Please also visit my author page to get more books in the Ruby & Billy series.

Ruby was a happy little girl.
She was always very busy.
Oh! There was so much to do!
Ruby had tosay hello to the butterflies in the garden.
Ruby had to chase the birds.
Ruby had to wash Bella the cat.
Ruby had to put flowers in Buddy's hair.

Oh yes! There was so much to do!
But sometimes things didn't go right.

Sometimes, when she said hello to the butterflies, she tripped on a stone!

Sometimes, when she chased the birds, her lovely hat flew off!

Sometimes—well, to be honest, all of the time—Bella the cat didn't want to be washed!

Sometimes, when she put flowers in Buddy's hair, he would give her a big kiss and knock her down!

When these things happened, Ruby wanted her binky.
Her binky was big and pink. It made her feel better.

Whenever she had a nap, Ruby had to have her binky.

If she didn't get it, she was upset.

Mom and Dad said to Ruby 'You're a big girl now. You don't need your binky anymore.'
But Ruby loved her big pink binky.

She was never EVER going to give it up.
'Will you give up your binky for a bowl of strawberry ice cream?' Mom asked.

Ruby would not give up her big pink binky for strawberry ice cream.

'Will you give up your binky for a trip to the park?' Dad asked.

Ruby would not give up her big pink binky for a trip to the park.

'Will you give up your binky for a butterfly sticker?' Gran asked.

Ruby would not give up her big pink binky. Not even for a butterfly sticker.

Ruby's brother Jake made fun of her. 'Ruby loves her binky,' he sang.
Yes, I do, Ruby thought.

Then Jade hid Ruby's bright pink jelly sandals. 'I'll show you where they are,' he said, 'if you give up your dummy.'

Ruby cried and cried. She loved her big pink dummy, but she loved her bright pink jelly sandals too.

Mum was cross with Jade and sent him to the naughty step.

'Stupid binky,' Jake grumbled from the naughty step. He had to tell Ruby where her pink jelly sandals were. She put them away and then crawled onto the couch for a nap.

All that worrying and crying was very tiring. She had her big pink binky in her mouth, of course.

Buddy saw that Ruby was sleeping. He jumped up on the couch too and snuggled beside her.

While she was sleeping—
her big pink dummy fell out of her mouth!

Ruby was upset when she woke up.
Where was her big pink dummy?

Jade must have taken it! But no, he was still on the naughty step.

It was Mommy! But no, she was in the kitchen making supper.

And then she saw Buddy in the garden, chewing something.
What was it?.......

Oh no! It was her big pink binky. Buddy dropped it on the ground.

Oh no! It was her big pink binky.
Buddy dropped it on the ground.

Oh dear! It was covered in yucky dog slobber!

And it had a tear in it!
Ruby was so mad!

Buddy gave her a big kiss to say sorry.

But Ruby just crossed her arms.

And pouted.

Then Buddy brought Ruby her teddy bear and dropped it in her lap.

Ruby looked down at the teddy bear.
She looked at Buddy.
What should she do?

She gave Buddy a BIG hug.
She felt better again. Ruby and Buddy snuggled up for a cuddle.

And she didn't need her binky to feel good.

She had Buddy.
And she had Jake, who was very sorry for being mean.
He helped her pop the yucky not-so-big and not-so-pink-anymore binky in the bin.
And you know, she wasn't a bit sad.

'Ruby no more binky' she said.

Thank you for reading……..

Please remember to leave a review if you enjoyed my book it would be nice to hear what you and your children thought of this book☺

Thank you for your time.

Pamela

If you enjoyed this book please also check out these books in the Billy, Ruby and Emergency Services Series below…..

  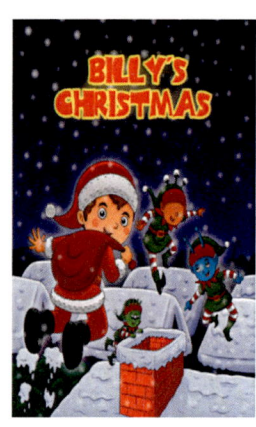 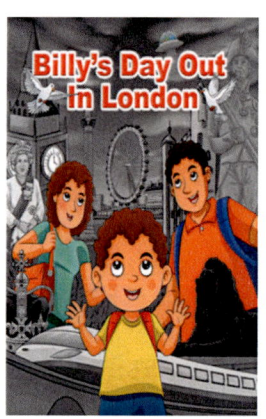 

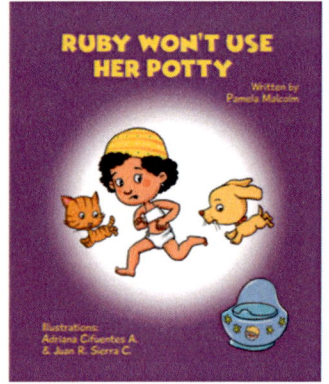  

Please visit Aryla Publishing for more books by Pamela Malcolm and other great Authors. Sign up to be informed of upcoming free book promotions and a chance to win prizes in our monthly prize draw.

Please visit [Aryla Publishing](#)
and Follow us on [Facebook](#) & [Twitter](#)
Thank you for your support!

Other children series published by [Aryla Publishing](#)

Author [Casey L Adams](#)
Body Goo 1 [Sneezing](#)
Body Goo 2 [Burping](#)
Body Goo 3 [Farting](#)
Body Goo 4 [Vomiting](#)
Body Goo 5 [The Crusty Bits](#)
Body Goo 6 [The Sticky Bits](#)
Love Bugs [Don't Step on The Ant](#)
Love Bugs [Don't Splat The Spider](#)

Also [Subscribe](#) to Billy's Monthly Vlog on Youtube to find out what he is up to.

New Vlogs every month

Made in the USA
San Bernardino, CA
26 July 2018